A FISH, A FROG AND A GNOME

My Favorite Poems

By Jennise Conley M.Ed.

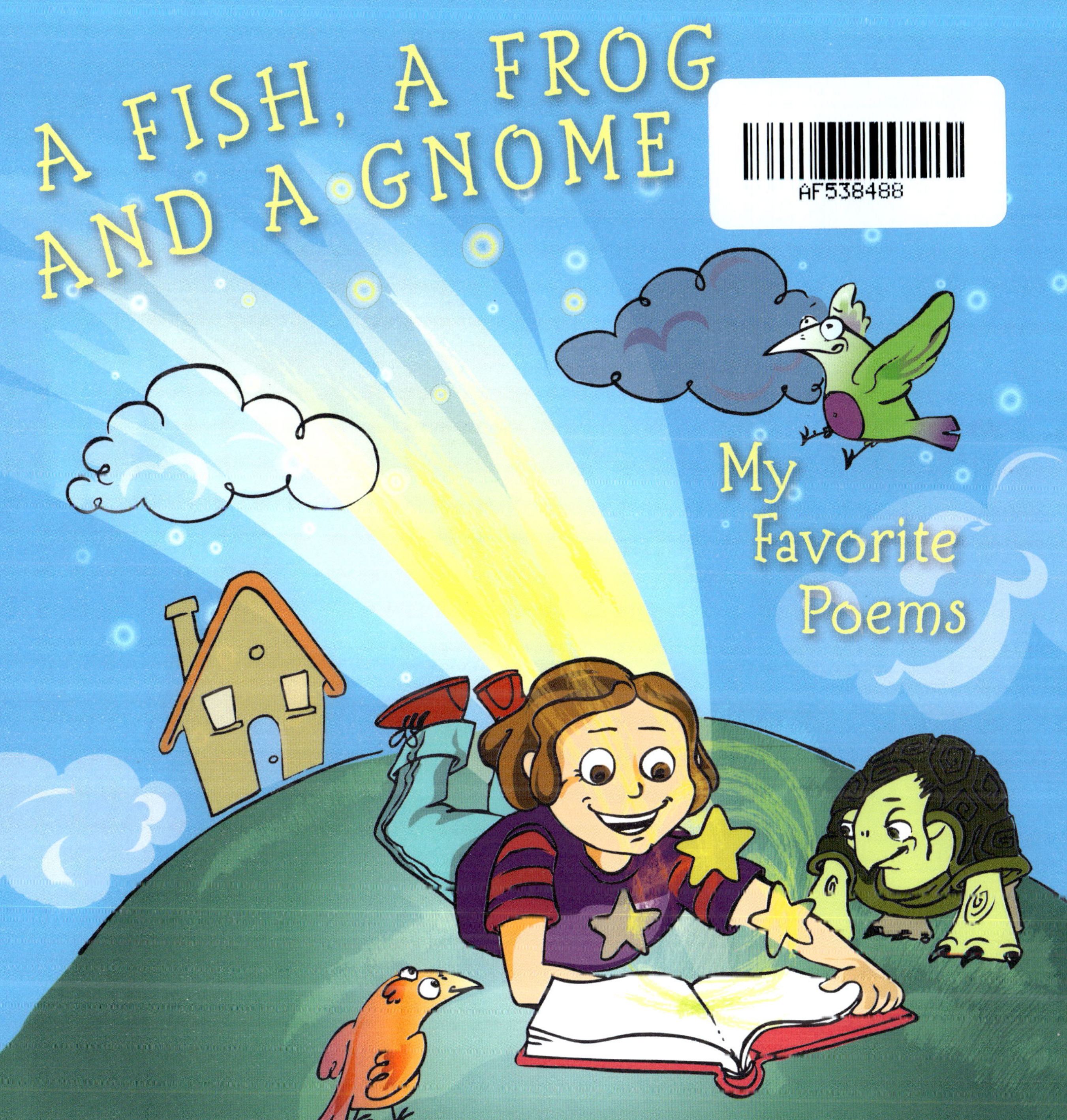

ISBN: 0615602975
ISBN 13:9780615602974
Library of Congress Control Number: 2012933479
Jennise\Conley, Goodyear, AZ

For my husband, family, friends, teachers, professors, and students.
Thanks.

How to Read This Book

Dear Parents,

The brain is most impressionable to the nuances of language during the first three years of life, so it is important to introduce story time long before your child expresses interest. If you portray books as a treasure trove of exciting mysteries and new ideas to discover, the magical world of books will become a natural part of your child's world. Starting an early ritual of reading is as simple as implementing what Doctor Jill Stamm defines as the ABCs of early brain development:

Attention—Even if five minutes is all you can afford, children need undivided attention during story time. When you are interested and enthusiastic, they are too.

Bonding—From the day they are born, children often find a parent's voice the most comforting sound in the world. Quality quiet time, free from life's distractions and modern technology, is the best way to create and reinforce feelings of love and security. When calm and relaxed, children are more receptive to learning.

Communication—Books expose children to things they rarely see, such as trains or elephants, which enhances concept development. Stories also introduce new topics to your child's world, providing prime opportunities to discuss sensitive subjects, such as sharing, sadness, or using hurtful words.

The Importance of Reading for Fun

From Dr. Seuss to Shel Silverstein, most beloved children's book authors are masters at playing with language. Following the lead of these brilliant storytellers, the fun rhymes contained in this book are based on rhythm and repetition, while the simplistic pictures are clear and colorful. These short verses and vibrant pictures are designed to teach the basic structure of the English language and develop memorization skills.

Even if children do not understand the words or pictures on the page, looking at books teaches them that symbols have meaning. As they develop an ear for the cadence of language, they also learn that letters strung together in various ways take on different meanings. Story time for young learners is not about learning how to read. Instead, focus on building vocabulary and increasing recognition of the everyday objects that fill your child's tiny world.

What Science Says about Reading

Although scientists have not established a consistent, direct link between early reading and later intelligence, child development experts agree rhyming poems improve cognitive abilities, such as processing information, understanding abstract concepts, making decisions, and solving problems.

A 1994 Head Start study revealed that children who are actively involved in stories through questions and observations are 93 percent more successful at linking letters and sounds. The key to dialogic reading, which hones comprehension, perception, and recollection skills, is asking questions such as, "What color is that truck?" or "What is this silly dog wearing?" You can also count similar objects or make predictions about what will happen next. The study concluded that the direct interaction between parent and child is the key to successfully learning language.

Additionally, Yale University researchers discovered hearing problems affect the brain's ability to distinguish subtle sound differences, thereby influencing reading and speaking skills. Reading aloud stimulates the neurons in the auditory cortex, the region of the brain responsible for processing sound. Meanwhile, early repetition of rhymes helps children develop phonemic awareness and improve memory recollection.

Ages and Stages of the Growing Brain

Although newborns cannot see colors or understand words, they can explore books through touch. Reading at this age is about bonding and comfort, so any material will work, whether it is a parenting magazine or a lengthy novel. During tummy time, flip through a simple picture book filled with black and white geometric shapes. Once baby can sit up, introduce lap reading.

Between six and eight months, vision is fully established and the brain is creating neural networks to understand rhythmic patterns in speech. Babies learn about the world by exploring with their hands and mouths, so offer cloth or plastic books that contain a variety of textures.

By twelve months, babies understand more words than they can speak, so focus on developing their receptive vocabulary. Turn grabby hands into productive ones by making your child the official book holder or page turner.

Between eighteen months and twenty-four months, introduce new books that are relevant to what your child is experiencing. You can also begin encouraging your child to choose his or her own books. Reading at this stage is not a linear experience, so let your child randomly choose the pages they want to read.

By age three toddlers are ready for books that label emotions, actions, and familiar people. To nurture pre-literacy skills, build upon the rhyme and rhythm of poetry by having your child create his or her own pictures or words to continue the story.

Tips and Tricks

The best way to avoid frustration is to keep story time a fun experience. Change your cadence, use silly voices for different characters, point to corresponding pictures as you read along, or try some of these simple tips to keep your child connected to the story.

Read before Nap Time and Bedtime

Weaving a reading regime into an already hectic schedule may seem nearly impossible. The good news is that preschoolers have short attention spans, so two, ten-minute sessions each day are enough to lay the foundation for a lifelong love of learning and reading. If you are too tired, ask older toddlers to tell you a story.

Balance Variety and Repetition

Reading the same story dozens of times may sound tiresome, but the brain enjoys familiarity through repetition and needs repeated exposure to the same ideas before that information is stored in the long-term memory bank. For your child, each reading reveals something different. Introduce new books by choosing topics that are relevant to your child's interests, or build upon familiar characters with fresh storylines. This will help your child build a relationship with books and, best of all, language.

Rhyme Time

This book has three delightful, whimsical rhymes about wishes. Talk about words that rhyme, point out rhyming words in your everyday world together, or encourage your child to add a verse to their favorite poem.

Sincerely,
Jennise Conley

Reference

Stamm, J. 2007. *Bright from the Start.* New York: Gotham Books.

1
2
3

The First Wish

I made a wish

to catch a fish

with worms that swish.

I caught a shoe

that looked like new.

I wish there were two!

The Second Wish

There once was a frog

DOGS

who sat on a log

and wished he was a dog.

Then came a fairy

who made him all hairy.

Now he's the dog-frog
of the prairie.

1
2
3

The Third Wish

In a quiet home,

you can find a gnome

sleeping on a piece of foam.

He wished for a bed,

but as he rested his head,

he found his pillow
was a loaf of bread.

The End

Energy and Sciences Education Initiative

A portion of the proceeds of this purchase will benefit the Energy and Sciences Education Initiative (ESEI). ESEI is a research and advocacy nonprofit for novel and contemporary learning methodologies in today's schools and educational programs. Its mission is to increase and improve energy education, environmental awareness, technology-enhanced learning, and media arts programs in today's education systems.

ESEI is using modern learning design to enhance child-centered educational theory and practice through a socio-technological approach. This nonprofit is working hard to promote current educational needs and conditions that will enhance today's curriculum and instruction practices. The Energy and Sciences Education Initiative believes that we must reject the one-size-fits-all educational solutions; rather, we must help each student learn at his or her own pace. ESEI is working hard to create education programs that are enhanced for better instruction and that are more engaging for our children.

Learn more about the Energy and Sciences Education Initiative at
www.ESAwareness.org

Made in the USA
Lexington, KY
07 May 2012